REA

PRAISE FOR MINTON SPARKS' WORKS

Sparks can render her South with bull's eye diction and down-home wit, but she also brings a clear eye to her own place in somebody else's story. Sparks knows the South's many undersides and voices.

> —Kathryn Stripling Byer, NC Poet Laureate and author of five books of poetry, including the award-winning *Wildwood Flower* (LSU Press)

With authentic voice and vivid image, Minton Sparks renders past, place, family, and community as sharply as an Exacto Knife. "I'll give you reality," the narrator claims in prelude to *Ambulance Chasers*. And in *Desperate Ransom* each character and each story comes from a place so real and sentient, you will wish it was your own history to remember. Each poem feels like the hard, tight, potent seed of a novel. Minton is a force of nature!

> —Darnell Arnoult, author of *Sufficient Grace* and
> *What Travels With Us: Poems*

Sparks talks like Lucinda Williams sings; low, bed-headed and husky with sin, either remembered or imagined. In the syncopated monologues on her new spoken-word album, THIS DRESS, your gas-pumping mama, your fellow Baptists and your unmentionable relatives occupy every slot on the Waffle House jukebox, and when musical guests like Keb'Mos' and Maura O'Connell chime in, you can even dance to 'em.

> —Jim Ridley *Nashville Scene*

With a voice born for gospel and a word artistry that makes you laugh and weep by turns, Sparks offers poems sorrowful and hilarious about the land of the double-wides.

> —*SANTA BARBARA INDEPENDENT*: June 2005

The Nashville poet and storyteller unearthed another set of wondrous vignettes that once again drew an unforgettable picture of life in the South. Sparks has a unique niche that soulfully marries the Southern storytelling tradition with the strains of old-time music for a hybrid that is all her own.

> —Mary Houlihan, *Chicago Sun Times*

There's no one quite like Sparks on the contemporary music scene—no one with her ability to find and describe the haunting rhythms of this world in such precise, unadorned terms.
—*PERFORMING SONGWRITER,* May 2004

THE TENNESSEAN, May 7, 2006
Rodney Crowell Sings Minton Sparks' praises
by Fiona Soltes

"Rodney Crowell is a fan. Not just any fan, mind you, but an unabashed, unapologetic, enthusiastic, gushing admirer of Minton Sparks. So much so that he once bought 60 CDs from the trunk of her car. 'I'm just captivated by language' he says. 'And Minton Sparks is a master." Some might say the same about Crowell; winner of a Grammy, an ASCAP Creative Acheivement Award and a spot in the Nashville Songwriter's Hall of Fame, he has his own share of devoted followers. And yet, for Crowell, taking part in "Minton Sparks & Friends@TPAC—The Voices of Today" Saturday is a chance to be 'close to greatness.'"

Desperate Ransom

Desperate Ransom
setting her family free

MINTON SPARKS

THOMAS NELSON
Since 1798

thomasnelson.com

The author gratefully acknowledges the editors of the following publications in which some of the poems herein first appeared, some in slightly different form: "Clackamas Literary Review," "Lonzie's Fried Chicken," "Anthology: Not Just Your Mother's Cookbook," "Anthology: Working Hard for the Money, America's working poor in stories, poems and photos."

Desperate Ransom

Published in Nashville, Tennessee by Thomas Nelson, Inc.

Thomas Nelson, Inc. titles may be purchased in bulk for educational, business, fund-raising, or sales promotional use. For information, please e-mail SpecialMarkets@ThomasNelson.com.

Library of Congress Cataloging-in-Publication Data

Sparks, Minton.
  Desperate ransom / Minton Sparks.
    p. cm.
  ISBN-13: 978-1-59554-262-5
  ISBN-10: 1-59554-262-0
  1. Southern States—Fiction. 2. Rural families—Fiction. I. Title.
PS3619.P354D47 2007
813'.6—dc22   2007003298

Printed in the United States of America

07 08 09 10 11 QW 6 5 4 3 2 1

For Addiesue and Billy Webb

Keep in mind, now, I used to hyperventilate every time I had to read Scripture out loud in Sunday school, so I might stumble a bit through this, my voice quivering along the way. It's important, though, for me to go back over things as they happened. In some way each family member is a colorful character in the book of Who I Am. When I tell their stories, I also tell mine. And I've got to tell it.

Think of it this way: We've invited the whole family over for Saturday night dinner. A piano bench and all the extra chairs from the back bedrooms are squeezed around that oval dining table with the maple finish; Momma had to set three extra leaves into the grooves to make it big enough for all of us cousins. The little ones will be sent down to card tables in the den, which is probably best for everybody since some of the stories have a Budweiser flavor that could stunt a growing mind.

Right now, Momma's over by the oven, wiping brow-sweat on her dishtowel. She's about to holler.

"Y'all hear me? Supper's on the table. Food's getting cold."

The iced tea's been poured and the stories will start to fly here in a second across Momma's soul food; anybody absent is fair fodder for slight slander. If you end up sitting at the spot where you have to straddle the table leg, please bear with me; nothing about the Sparks family was ever straight and narrow (though I think just about everybody except Terri Diane has been baptized). Sometimes a tale will sound more like a poem or a song or a speech, just depending upon who rears up in my head to tell it. Still, I'm going to let every one of these characters say their piece, no matter how long it takes. Well, it looks like we're all just about ready to say "Amen."

All right now, let me catch my breath.

Here goes.

Primary Resistance

I sassed her, and in some ways
I'm still paying for it.
Lanky and tall, I lick my lips
to grease the skids, slide
across the line of lost innocence.
I peel her damp dishwater hands
from my face, hands born
to yank cow teats, snap pole beans.

Gertrude grows on people,
or at least she tries to.
A jumber-jaw and protruding mole
form a face like a clumsy letter Q ,
or a slightly-Slavic Reverend Billy Graham.

I draw a breath from my quiver
and let it fly: "You are not my aunt,
Gertrude. Do you hear me?
Not blood kin."

Pentecostal buns nearly come undone.
Ice sweats uncomfortably in mason jars.
I speak the truth:
Gertrude is no relative.
She is Mee Maw's best friend.
This is their ritual, not mine.

Every Saturday, planted like boxwoods
around the small kitchen table,
they snack on hot homemade
fried peach pies
and cold, sweetened
Lipton iced tea.
Talk till noon.

They return to pretend,
smooth over rumpled dresses
and my words.
Grandmother reminds: "Young lady,
that dress you're wearing was a gift,
store-bought for you by your
Aunt Gertrude—thankless child."

The moment is mapless.
I am fresh preserves between these
two doughy crusts.

I refill their teas (overfull),
wipe glass-sweat on my flowerdy shorts,
salute the now *"Mrs. Frazier"* adieu,
avoid the serpent slits
of my grandmother's eyes,
and stride,
stride
          through the door
                    to ride my bike.

Pilgrimage to Aunt Virginia's

Cheese and crackers litter the floorboard of the silver Eldorado.
Air is car-travel stale, an odor like feet.
When the dust clears from our labored turn into the gravel lot,
six emerge—sophisticates against the front porch of a failing country store.
An electric Co-Cola sign, a swinging screen door between worlds.
The sign don't lie; green bottles cool in a chin-high metal box inside.
We pass rows of waving Nilla Wafers on the shelves.

In the back of the store a sinister room lures us:

A flaking, putrid
pink-skinned woman
decays in a four-poster bed.
Eyes the size of chicken eggs
that could have been
laid this morning
and sold this afternoon.
Her head sways there,
sweats a dirty pillow.
Grand Ole Opry
on the radio.
The near-song she sings
isn't celebration—

"If you're happy and you know it nod your head."

It's desperate, like crying:
"I'm out on Plymouth
sitting on a rock."
The pilgrim fires her line
buckshot into our New World.

We take it in the chest, faceless relatives shuffling around her bed
embarrassed to acknowledge this specter.
Uncle Brother offers me a brush to stroke the death hair.
I imagine years will clump out into my hands.
I cling there to the roof of my mouth and my mother's leg.

Line Up

"Y'all line up!" Mee Maw hollered
intending to willow-whip us all.
Her words ghost-stung, red wasps
against my gangly legs.

She lined us up
beside her school bus,
the one she drove at daybreak
to earn her *own* money.

I was standing so close
to each of my criminal cousins
we were strangling
each other's shadows.

"Which one of you wants it first?"
Again the terrorist demands.
Much like you, none of us
raised our hands.

"Playing down in that ditch?
Right where the neighbor lady landed?"
Thump. "In a nest of snakes—
land sakes, child."

Bewildered, not brave,
I reach for the sky
with my left hand.
"Whip me; I'll go first."

In my boldness, confused for courage,
she recognizes her line,
and it will *not* be broken.
I. Am. Her. Own.

$\mathcal{Y}$ou never know what will happen; you just never know. Mee Maw was the Cleanliness-Is-Next-to-Godliness type. She believed "Thou Shalt Maintain Near-Sterile Hygiene" and "Thou Shalt Always Be Prepared" (later borrowed by the Boy Scouts of America) to be the eleventh and twelfth scriptural commandments. However, in the eyes of the other side of our family, the amount of money Mee Maw spent on Comet, Windex, and Pine Sol was clearly criminal. All the children and grandchildren heard many a supper-table sermon on Attention to the Little Things—things like the state of our undergarments—since unforeseen calamity and misfortune undoubtedly awaited us.

Sadie Ramsey, the neighbor lady, proved the gravity of Mee Maw's maxim after a tornado blew her plumb up into a tree late one night. Miss Sadie's nephew, Howard Jr., in a state of shock, stumbled house to house announcing her disappearance. The folks on Deadfall Road formed a posse to search the surrounding area. It wasn't long before we heard some moaning and groaning, and a little humming of the hymn "Jesus Calls Us O'er the Tumult." Sure enough, there was Miss Sadie, wedged into the V of a multi-armed oak, way high up in that tree.

Best I can remember we all huddled up around the base, some of us holding hands for emotional support, our heads reared back, necks straining to assess the damage. I must admit that, to our horror, the worst of what we saw wasn't the bloody cuts or blooming bruises poor Sadie bore. No, what shocked us most was the tattered and holey underwear she wore.

That singular sight of raggedy, extra-large, cream-colored Carter-brand panties threw our grandmother into a tizzy from which she's never truly recovered. Later, when we got home, all hell broke loose. Mee Maw started cleaning her already spotless home like out-of-state company was coming. She mopped all the floors, scoured the small bathroom, twice, and put fresh doilies out under all the lamps. At the climax of her cleaning frenzy, she took a hidden wad of money from a shoebox on the closet shelf, hopped on the bus and headed downtown to Cain-Sloan's department store. A few hours later she returned with the nicest pair of silk drawers that money could buy: cobalt blue with a wide lace around the legs, all wrapped up in fancy tissue paper.

And to this very day, anytime the sky looks threatening or the winds get high, Mee Maw steals off to her bedroom dresser and steps into what are now affectionately referred to by all of us as: "Mee Maw's Tornado Drawers."

Words of Wisdom

"Time changes nothing girl
but the size of your underwear . . . and hopefully your hairdo."

Mee Maw painted a red stripe
down the street side of the barn
every time her daughter
married another man.

Beneath her labored breath
I heard her six times say,
"Just like Aunt Lottie, just like her!
Married seven and died a pauper."

Dipping her brush
into the blood-red paint
she turns her heavy prophesy
on me:

"You girl, you'll end up in a double-wide,
sure as shooting—five at your feet, dust
fogging the white sheets
you keep hanging out to dry."

Mississippi Moonshine

She'd a' been the first issued a DUI
on the Mississippi,
my Gypsy used to say.

Out on the bow
of a muddy Mississippi barge
on a sweltering Delta night
Thelma ached for an anchor.
Nipping hidden moonshine
beneath a cloud of weary.

Been cooking in the kitchen
since sun up, ankles swollen
beyond the banks of her shoes.
The dark drank the color
from her yellow hair as it fell
oily in whiskey curls
around her once beautiful face.

Thelma was cursed by extremes:
beauty, a penchant for strong anything,
and barge-kitchen men.

Drunk, driving right down
the middle of the muddy waters,
she begged the sky a favor.
The answer came on moonshine fumes
written against the night:

Being too much of yourself needs no forgiveness.

Killin' Time

I still feel uncomfortable when I tell it:
Brother and I killin' time nibbling snake grass

in the front yard, waiting on the Bible school bus.

The sour weeds grew right there where the gutter rusted through.
Baptists borrowed the bus from our primary school,

kept it on Pastor's lawn all summer long.

It was hot as the dickens. We filled water balloons to sip on or throw at.
Brother busted one on my back, a perfect circle, balloon water and sweat.

I knelt there at the spigot fumbling to fill a green one

the color lightening to lime as the fragile skin swelled with water.
I tried to tie the knot twice, but it slipped from my hands.

Yeah, it did. Boy, just slipped right out.

Next, I hear his sandals lickety-split through dry grass
like a struck match gonna burn our house down

sprinting after a swollen red balloon rolling into the road.

Durn slick sandals, blood-blistered feet.
They say he darted into her blind spot, caught the front tire.

Neighbor told me later that driver-woman was a wreck.

I   screamed   bloody murder for the ice cream
they'd cranked at church. Don't matter now. It all melted.

Wouldn't nobody eat after he ran into the street like that.

One summer, Momma unloaded more makeup than anybody else in her territory, which included both Sumner and Humphreys counties. Outside the long arm of the department stores, women went wild over the Mary Kay line of cosmetics. Momma had certain concealers on back order for months, the kind that reflect light and reduce circles under your tired eyes. Ona May Weatherman told somebody that Momma was in line to win one of those fin-backed Cadillacs the company gave away to their highest selling reps. What she didn't know was that Momma had blown by her quota weeks earlier and that the car was already on its way to our driveway.

Momma was motivated. Daddy didn't allow her out of the house alone, except to grocery shop or make a little money peddling those special soaps and lotions to her friends at home-thrown Mary Kay parties. When she walked back into the house he'd make a "grease-my-palm" motion—rubbing one hand against the other—so he could take the bulk of the money away from her. He'd store the cash in a cigar box under his side of the bed until betting season arrived; then he'd pull the wad of bills out from its hiding place and start running numbers on college football games.

What I neglected to tell Daddy, because he never asked, was that Momma was socking away savings down the neck of his old combat boot up top of the hall closet every time we came home from a Mary Kay party. I think he might have finally figured it out, though, that day she sped away, pelting the front porch with dirt and pebbles spun up from the steel-belted radials on that brand new pink Mary Kay car.

Screaming Around Corners

My momma flies a car.
Black gloves, wings
on the wheel
of a long silver bird,
lightning fast.
Brother and I burn
    fingernails across red leather Cadillac seats.
"Hang on, sister!"

Her world: four white walls
    — *Whitewalls* —
a box that rounds sharp corners.
Momma squeals at demons
I haven't yet met.
    Errrrrrk
Cackling witch—
like speed
is the next best thing to love.
Windows down, hair afire.
    She
        is close
            to free.

Nosy neighbors snoop
behind heavy curtains.
Click.
Flash.
Pictures developed
into fence-row gossip:
"She mowed down my Maple."
"Maimed my tomatoes."
"Totaled the swing-set and never looked back."

Shhhhhh.

Momma bribes our silence
with Juicy Fruit gum,
"Don't you tell your daddy."
Tires still squall, rubber
marks the road.
Her alibi:
    "They need more air."

I turn the corner
on adolescence, aching
to burn my own rubber
behind the wheel.
A gray Skylark four-door arrives.
I too will fly,

only toward my life,
                   not away.

Hell's Kitchen

Mid-August, muggy heat.
The devil fries some meat
up on the stove.
Window fans hum,
stir the misery —
can't none of us
get a dance off to this.

After killing flies
with a splattered swatter,
sister sins: washes her filthy hands
in Satan's clean kitchen sink.
Skint knees always sting
after red brick and brimstone
on the floor.

Steam rises off supper,
curls across salmon croquettes,
butter beans, and corn bread,
our wild ache for warmth answered in the air.

Old Scratch lifts a heat-trapped prayer:
"Never eat the good Lord's food upset."
Stone-cold deaf, we dig
in the deep of our food
afraid we'll be late
for Sunday night church school.

Reaching across the table
for anything,
I knock over my tea glass.
It darkens Her floors,
stings my thighs;
I freeze in the stoplights
of those rage-red eyes.

Beelzebub'll blister me—
She flies into a fiery fit.
Six scorched horses rear
away from the fire
to make way for the mop
thrust in like a pitchfork
to sop up the mess.

A costume change is called for,
my thrift-store shorts
soaking wet.

That night at training union
after Kool-Aid, crackers,
and a simple circle game:
"We All Fall Down,"
Dotty Taylor teaches
the lesson about Lucifer—
God's favorite angel
'til he fell
out of heaven into hell.
A fallen angel.

I think of Momma's face
and how it fell, fierce
after Daddy drove away
and left us, and how we
all
fall
down.
Fallen angels,
get your butts back up.
Try again, and again,
one more time.

$\mathcal{I}$n the week leading up to our annual Florida beach trip to Daytona, over the loud pops of her gum-wad and the wrinkling sound of packing sleeves of peanut butter crackers into the cooler, Aunt Wardeen would admonish us.

"Y'all get outside and knock a little of that white off your legs. You look sickly."

The infamous Base Tan was extolled as extremely important to survival in our community. The thinking seemed to be: if you go out and ruin your skin just a tad before you get to the beach, it won't ruin so bad when you're actually lying under the blazing hot sun on your Dr. Pepper beach towel, listening to K.C. and the Sunshine Band on the portable player, pounding peanut butter and jelly sandwiches and cans of Coke. Those searing rays, reflecting off the salt water, might somehow be kinder to your pre-toasted skin.

This was back when the only sunscreen we had was a tube of nasty yellow paste with a baby blue cap. Momma'd smear the goo onto the tops of my shoulders and the bridge of my nose, the rest of my body left to fend for itself. Once that slathering took place I could pretty much play all day with my sisters on the beach. That is, until nighttime when I'd get the fried shrimp dinner over at Marco's Heritage Inn and a slight fever, my new Daytona T-shirt stinging my burnt back so bad I had to take it off on the way home.

Over the years I got older but only a little wiser in the ways of darkening my lily-white body. To call a girl "pasty white" or "fish-belly white" was slander, a real slap in the face. Nice creamy skin was not something we aspired to. I remember longing for a way to get a tan deep enough to last into the following summer so I wouldn't have to go back to square one the next year.

The prize at the end of the tanning rainbow was Hawaiian Tropic Gold Label, a thick bronzing oil that smelled of coconuts and Florida, rubbed-in by a wheeler-dealer lifeguard sporting white teeth and rurnt skin. We high school girls would hang on his every word of advice about the best tanning products and procedures, while Earth, Wind & Fire songs blared on his 8-track player in the background. Our guru's recommended protocol required ascending a progressive ladder of tanning oils over a ten-day to two-week period, products he just so happened to sell out of the back of his gold Camaro. Being of Scotch-Irish descent, and in a great hurry to win his affections with my emerging Sophia Loren skin tone, I had real trouble with the patience of this application.

As I look back, I see I really should have had my butt beaten for not staying with the level 45 sunscreen. Instead, I'd slather on the Silver Label tanning oil by day two, way before I was ready, and burn myself to a crisp. Scorching my skin into cooked-lobster pink around the tender edges of my green polka-dotted bathing suit left me sitting up at night, in the hotel room bathtub in a vinegar soak, my mother sloppily slapping on the Solarcaine.

Childhood Paints: A Tennessee/Florida Canvas

Daddy haunts this blue beach. His cologne:
fishy heat. Condominiums,
black pepper along the shore.

He abandoned us to build them, stacked
greenbacks in a small bank. Saltwater
soaked him, heavy the walk home.

Or did he just hate being with her?
They never divorced. An ivory moon
his companion, night after night,

oily martinis over an aqua shimmer.
In his palm he held the thin string
that threaded the pulley of the moon.

His wife yanks a willow branch, blisters
our bottoms. My pigtail braid
stretched from sea to Tennessee.

Her tug drew the rope back
across the moon, it broke over his balcony,
a backdrop that blood-reds his children's lives.

This distant town, a home I never
wanted, still hauls gray waves to shore.
Waves that towed Daddy

to white-capped breasts,
a reluctant tide. Always adrift
inland, in my mother's house.

I Thought He Might Kill Her

When the lock box was empty
and the savings bond gone
we kids watched him make her march —
a grown woman now —
across the Formica under fluorescents
to the kitchen table for questioning.
"Where's my money, housewife?"
A cancer stick drips from his bottom lip.
"Our money, Hon'."

His eyes knock at her
like a bore-bee on a barn beam.
She studies her liver-spotted hands,
picks smooth cuticles 'til they bleed.
Our supper sits
on the black eye of the stove.
"Dumb Cluck, what were you thinking?"

Fay, her sister, was hungry,
the young'uns sickly,
yard-dogs starved.
He won't hear it, keeps a comin'.
She eases off the chair
wild eyes trained on faded seat fabric
like it was the one hollering.
Tiptoes to the toilet.
"Don't you walk away!"
The bathroom door clicks like a tomb.

She hisses into the mirror: "I hate him."
Hinges squeak on the medicine cabinet,
a plastic bottle with pink and blue writing
hits, rolls along cold white tile.
She floats back to her assigned seat
beside the stove,
cooks him dead in the eye.

Before long the bottle of Benadryl
kicks her head like a mule.
The dull thud against the table
sours my stomach.
Hell-raisin' ain't over
'til the ambulance arrives.

Don't none of us know
if she meant to take that much
off him or not.

In this one, we're all there in our home theater, the upstairs hallway, a big bowl of popcorn soaked in a sickening amount of butter. Daddy projects, in moving pictures, Momma's grandmother, Susie, black and white onto the bathroom door. She's held captive up there, pinned in that dour dress to a wingback chair by a long row of hot bulbs and a handheld camera. Momma said she never spoke again after her youngest died at five years old, a mute mother to the remaining seven.

Without moving my mouth, I read her like a book.

Susie squint-stares into the light like she's consenting to go blind, half-heartedly flops her wrist back and forth, a good-bye wave and obligatory smile. There in the hallway the trapped clackety-clack noise of the reel-to-reel drives me wild. I cup my hands over my ears but things only amplify. In my head Great-grandmother Susie screams bloody murder, the camera right up on her. You can see in her face all the words she won't say and all the tears she can't cry. I remember Momma's warning: "Be careful what you watch; pictures'll penetrate you to the bone" (though, I suppose, her admonition might have been a lesson against nasty movies at the downtown theater).

I want to yank open the bathroom door or cut a hole into that makeshift wooden screen, big enough to set dumb Susie free. I'm afraid if I stare at her wordless life any longer she might stay trapped way down deep inside of me.

Bird in a Cage

Sitting on the sofa beside
Great-aunt Evie she quotes me a line
from her favorite movie: *It's a sin to kill a*
mockingbird 'cause all it wants to do is sing. Uncle
Sam was a singer before he was drafted. Now he's a stray
bull, cross-fenced on an unfamiliar battlefield—so sick of the sight
of blood he can't castrate the hogs. The farm is *rurnt*. His
coal-black cowlick stands on end as he faces the wind and
the rest of life without a leg. Limb lopped off in a for-
eign war, never figured out what he was fight-
ing for. Now his mind wanders foxholes as he
strangles the neck of his guitar. Sam crossed those
waters against his will. Made a living 'til then off a moonshine still, sweet songs, copper coils, a Mississippi moon. He'd
fly all over a pinewood stage; now music only fuels the rage as he
cocks that angry arm, saws twilight in two.
Might as well slug foothills with his fists for all the good his anger
does him. They'll never make *a solid soldier out of a song-bird*, Evie'd
say—mad enough to fight a circle-saw. By the end of her telling my
ankles are swelling and a dawn breaks across her mourning face.
She lays the story's end out like a steaming hot breakfast: cat-head
biscuits, bacon strips, and muscular coffee. She turns and rattles
the bars of my two stick arms, realizing: "I've lived my life in the
pen that war put around your Uncle. Now, ain't that low-down?"

Sin-Sick Soul

They do it in the grade school infirmary,
'cause she keeps the clinic twice a week.

He's a Church of Christ deacon,
and president of the Ruritan.
She's a V.P. of the D.A.R.
A match made in heaven—

except he's already married
and thirty years her senior.

Now I lay me down to sleep
with a married man I meet
at the ice cream social.

"The word *fool*," Momma warned,
"is the devil's."

Wanda hangs her young life
on the empty promise
that Roy'll leave his wife.

He says might as well blow a hole
in his head, better off dead,
than sic the dog of divorce
on his soul.

Tongues of hellfire lick him,
fellow deacons warn him
about the wages of adultery
and all that.

Bleached blonde and sin-sick,
Wanda wads a would-be wedding dress
into a big box in her back seat.
The Chrysler careens
down the slick road to perdition.

Beneath her tires comes the crunch—
near-innocent box turtles instinctually
cross the road.

Turning in,
her lights pump the humps
up the gravel drive.
Love'll make a mess of these two.

Roy sulks in his white truck,
before he scratches off across the cornstalks,
dead at odd angles,
his hot hand heavy
on a cold revolver.

Cuckold-burrows cling to her nylons,
she's clutching empty handfuls
of old-man-door-handle
when the gun goes off—
his self-serving sacrifice
splatters his rearview mirror.

She swears in the deposition
it was never his heart's intention
to stick that pistol in his mouth.

A gun to his head,
he was better off dead
than sic the dog of divorce
on his soul.

I saw her one Sunday
on the church-house steps
rockin', and a cryin', dabbing
at her chest with the hem
of that faded, old wedding dress.

A gun to his head,
she's better off dead
than sic the dog of Love
on her soul.

The worst part about it was they were neighbors. And when you think of everything his wife Martha went though, it's no wonder she ended up like she did. Just hours after Roy blew his brains out she was up at the house waiting on the undertaker, eating the onionskin pages of Ephesians. No lie, she was killing time boiling Bible verses, stirring 'em like a stew. Never seen anything like it. Given enough time, she might have chewed right through Galatians.

All those years living in that big house at the end of the road, playing the part of ignorant wife, drove her 'round the bend. Before that final trouble she liked to collect Green Stamps, lick 'em and stick 'em in her book. She'd had her eye on a new mahogany-colored end table come Christmas.

Funny, but what'd made Martha most mad that day was not the sheriff scraping his muddy boots across her new-scrubbed porch, nor the deputy's bad breath hanging on his hateful words, but the dull sound of furnace pipes knocking and the squeals of the lusty hogs rutting in the side yard.

Didn't surprise me in the least bit, though, the way she fought when the EMTs arrived. It took three strapping men to bring Martha out of that house, and even then in a straitjacket. As they ushered her to the van, she was muttering some sing-song Scripture from Isaiah she'd learned by heart.

I can see her now, those large work hands neatly picking seed ticks off her white socks. Last time I stuck my head in to check on her, she was boiling in the heat of a hand-knit sweater and the steam up off a pot on the stove. Seems like she was born to live a life of leftovers.

Trella's Trash

Blind in one eye
and can't half see out the other.
Momma's favorite aunt was Trella,
so they called us when she left him.

"Trella's trash."
Kin folk punctuate the line
with pork-rind fingers.
"She finally up and left him."

Leaving-lies, told Arkansas-style,
hiss across the party line.
"She's sleeping with the help
at the nursing home
every time she visits her momma."

"How dare she leave."
"Sixty-five years of marriage;
sixty-five."
"Ninety-one and blind;
umm, umm."

Buck-naked, bare-boned
under that frayed housecoat,
she tripped over it
as she sprawled
into the backseat of the cab
hauling a handful
of wild daisies from the yard
clear across Little Rock.

I'd heard he beat her,
treated her like a slave,
made her tape Reynolds Wrap
over every peeling window
in that rundown house.
To keep out the Light.
He kept it out all right.
'Til dark was the only hand
Trella had to hold.

Ten years back she'd fired a shot
at Frank's Ford window,
gravel flying,
insulting the bruises
already staining her cheeks.

The hell she did.

That rifle kicked.
She sang "Amazing Grace"
into the smoke she casually blew
off the barrel of the gun.
She'd won,
for a minute.

Late that night
he was rattling the door.
"You want some more, Trella?
You want some more?"

"Sure I do, Frank.
                    Always did."

I believe that once you're eligible for the senior citizen discount down at the Martin Double movie theater, it's high time you and your sister stop dressing like identical twins. Durrell and Maydell Harding have dismissed my thoughts on this summarily. I know this to be true because, not long ago, I saw them parading through the parking lot in matching black-and-white-checkered cowboy shirts, making a beeline for a rerun of *Walking Tall*, that film about Tennessee's own Buford Pusser, each of them carrying a bag of home-popped popcorn into the theater, which, by the way, is against theater company policy. And a couple Sundays ago they marched into church service wearing identical light pink jumpers with flat shoes dyed to match.

Now, I'd feel bad talking about them this way, and if they hadn't been the ones to write the book on gossip, I wouldn't. However, if you could have heard those two at the yard sale the other day, talking to Luna Bugg (who I might mention, still push-mows her acre lot), you'd have heard more tales told out of school than you can count. Just like old biddies in a hen yard.

Cluck Cackle Peck

"Poor ole Darryl," biddies cluck
over crackling Co-Colas. "Linda's let herself go."

They peck, peck, popcorn
from a Tupperware bowl, and cackle.

"She's big as the broad-side of a barn."
"And he ain't but that big around."

"Won't wear a girdle."
"Can't keep house."

Squawking slows as they scratch at dirt
for a dropped kernel of corn.

"Those filthy house cats she keeps . . ."
"Somebody oughta call the law."

"My boy Sam saw her soldering *car parts*
into sculptures in the night sky."

"And there's Darryl breaking his back
on the graveyard shift."

"Oh, she'll be the death of Darryl . . .
mark my word." "Now girls, I heard

they caught her over at the song leader's house
bumping-uglies to Chet Atkins records."

"Nothing but gossip." "Well, I wouldn't touch
the wicked woman with a Jesus sanctioned ten-foot-pole."

"Wipe the dust from your feet girls, the dust
from your feet. Linda's let herself go."

These clucked curses—chicken mess—
only fertilize Linda's leaving.

Oh, they'd liked to've had a fit
the night she hiked her skirt and lit

out of that two-bit, dumb-cluck town.
By the grace of God that woman let herself go.

I mean to tell you . . . she let *Herself* go.
Yeah . . . let Herself go alright.

Go, Linda. Go, go, go!!

Dance Caller at the Grand Opening
Marco Polo Theme Park — 1973, Daytona Beach, Florida

Single-file
     Injun-style
Grab your honey
     and go hog-wild!

He lumbers from the men's room
to the gazebo stage
across a steamy parking lot.

Square wire glasses
oil-slip down his nose
as he fiddles
with the zipper
on his square-dance pants.

Behind him, a herd
of teenagers tote duffel bags,
Rutherford County Square Dancers
embossed on the side.

Their tap shoes
click-shuffle off-stage
like shod horses on hot pavement.
Clip-clop. Here they come.

Bluegrass blares
a high lonesome wail:
> *Shuffle one two*
> *Shuffle one two*

Dance caller hollers:
Swing your partner

Put the birdie in the cage
Birdie out and the old crow in
> *Old Crow back in the circle again*

The red rises on his face
as Penny Burns' dotted-swiss dress
slashes at storm skies.
Ricky Reed's wingtips
knock pockmarks
into asphalt.

Sweat runs creeks
down our backs
from the foothills of Tennessee.

    Yippee!

In the distance
a rollercoaster
crests the hill
        then
            falls.

Sweat-slick hands send me sprawling.
Pass the ladies on through
    Now gents, you too
        Circle back and howdy do!

The caller mops his brow
with a sweat-soaked red bandana.
    Shuffle one two
    Shuffle one two

Betty Blalock's bouncing bosoms
make a yes-man
of the hot clapping crowd.

When the time comes
for the buckdance
we hear:
    Clap, clap
        clap, clap, clap
    Clap, clap
        clap, clap, clap

Steve Buckner's up first with a self-styled
Appalachian stomp.
Gregg Webb hitches his britches
mule kicks, drops to splits
back up —
    Shuffle one two
        Howdy do!

The caller wails,
his face a splotched tangle
of sweat and distress.
Promenade
    Prome
        nade
    Ever'
        body pro
            me
                nade

It is then that the rain begins to fall,
a nearby popcorn awning too small
to shelter the sweltering crowd.
Some of us don't see him
crumble over his soft belly
holding the microphone.

We dance on.

The caller falls
into sticker bushes beside the stage,
clutches his checkered chest in a rage
from the heat and strain
and mumbles something like:

Shuffle one
    two

Shuffle one
    two

That ole boy got a pacemaker after all the heart trouble. Must have worked pretty well, too, because he was back up at the microphone the very next year to call the Sumner County Turkey Trot. Now that's a good time. And I can tell you right now what the problem is with today's young people; they can't find nothing better to do than to lock eyes on the television screen—*CSI: Wherever* or some "reality" show. I'll give you reality. Whatever happened to the good old days when on nights like this, during the middle of dinner, you might hear a faint siren in the distance? Daddy would slam his chair back from the table, pretending like he was going to take off his belt and whip one of us. But next thing you knew he was leading the charge to run and pile up in the car shouting, "We're going ambulance chasing!"

I remember one evening hanging onto a cyclone fence while a wrecker hauled the mangled body of a Buick LeSabre to the lot. You could see matted auburn hair pasted up onto the dashboard.

Now that was adventure.

Ambulance Chasers

After supper, rain rattles;
tears bead and slip down
a caulked kitchen window.
Dirty dishes drown
in a stainless-steel sink.

Our phone rumbles twice.
Sandy asks, "Can you spend the night?"
Momma nods *Yes* from the icebox;
a butter-dish slips,
strikes the floor.

Upstairs I pack my overnight case:
hairbrush, clean panties,
Waylon Jennings playing cards.
I wait in the garage
and pet the dog
'til they come.

A rusted-out truck arrives;
Sandy's stepdaddy drives.
We lounge on a Budweiser-
stained mattress in the back,
talk about boys.

Backing out,
her momma mouths,
Knock if you need us,
just knock
before she pops a top,
guzzles, chokes, and sputters.

Bonanza Steakhouse —
T-bones and Tater Tots.
I say I haven't eaten but I have.
Highway 50 fights us
like a wet cat locked in a dollhouse.
I'm carsick
way before the U-turn.

Come to find out,
these folks follow ambulances,
track trouble,
lap up flashing red lights
like malt liquor.
Lowlife snakes, we slither
toward the lake,
finally fishtail
to a stop.

Dizzy on stepdaddy's driving
I spin out onto the first dead body I ever saw —
stinking, fish-white beneath a sheet.
"Dead for days," the policeman says
like he's underwater.
They slide the bloated body
into the salivating siren-box.
Soaked, Sandy and I stand there and
split a Sprite.

I can't honestly tell my momma
in the morning
that I had a nice time.

Fear was the cornerstone upon which Uncle Charles built a life in the small town of two thousand five hundred legal residents. Born with a clubfoot, he felt a certain vulnerability that the rest of us must have sidestepped. Uncle Charles was fixated on danger. He fed his fascination by ingesting a steady diet of heinous crimes on television news shows. He was obsessed with the local case of Mandy Truman, a young girl abducted while selling Girl Scout cookies in her neighborhood; on the national level he found serial killer Jeffrey Dahmer spellbinding.

Now that I'm older, I see that his behaviors reflect a propensity for unwarranted precautions in the face of seemingly benign situations. But back then I admired his paranoid qualities. Although he was employed by Firestone Tire Company, to me he seemed like a prudent deputy sheriff or, even better yet, a secret agent. One evening, for instance, right around dusk, Uncle Charles drove out to get some Purity Milk and Wonder Bread at the Quick Stop convenience store. Before he left, he sat down on the ottoman, laced up his special shoe, then pulled his navy car coat off the nail by the door. Right before he hobbled out, though, he doubled back to unplug the receiver and its cord from the telephone and hide it up under his arm before he made his way outside.

This is the gospel truth. I know because that night he let me ride with him, provided I sat in the back and ducked down. When we got to the car, parked half a block away, he started it up and we drove off. He and Aunt Inez lived on Main Street near the square, a typically busy thoroughfare. Anytime another car pulled up beside us, he'd put the red receiver to his ear like he was in the middle of a conversation with somebody on the other end. He made gestures with his hands and moved his mouth but never made a sound. After he'd talked awhile, he'd hand the receiver over to a life-size blow-up doll perched in the passenger side seat. The doll wore a woman's white Sunday hat. He held the phone up to the place on its plastic head where an ear ought to be. When I asked him about the phone, he casually explained that it was just a "safety precaution." Uncle Charles drove a hunter green Fleetwood Cadillac which he felt made him a sitting duck for some sort of assault. His assumption seemed to be that no one would try to hurt him or his fancy car if he was accompanied and in constant phone contact with the outside world.

The safety charades didn't stop there. Uncle Charles would not park his cars in front of his own house for fear of drawing undue attention. He owned identical Fleetwoods, one for him and one for Aunt Inez. Most nights, he'd shuffle out to his car after dark and drive over a couple of streets to park in front of someone else's house. Same thing with Aunt Inez's vehicle. It would take him about thirty to forty-five minutes to situate the cars for the night. He also believed it to be crucial to vary the placement of the autos each time. He alleged that if the Cadillacs were sitting out in front of his modest house on Main, and some stranger was driving through town, the cars would make the house a target for crime, unspeakable acts of deviance and degradation to which he would not chance risking the virtues of Aunt Inez, nor the dogs. At the time, it made perfect sense to me.

The only time I really got into any sort of tangle with Uncle Charles was the night I worked parking cars in his side yard. The house was right across the street from a community college campus. My cousins and I used to park cars in their side lot to make money during the big concerts at the Auditorium. We could bank up to $100 each and then turn the rest of the cash over to Uncle Charles and Aunt Inez. But one time the Statler Brothers drove up in a limousine needing a safe place to stow their fancy automobile. Uncle Charles was inside the house. Without asking him, I allowed the mega country stars to park in Aunt Inez's dried-up wildflower garden for a flat fee of two hundred and fifty dollars. Uncle Clubfoot must have seen their long hair and cowboy dusters from the kitchen window. He barreled out of that house with a shotgun, ready to blow their heads off.

"Get off my property, you bunch of long-haired dope addicts!" he shouted, firing two shots into the air. He looked at me, shaking his head.

"You can't never trust somebody looks like that," he warned.

South of Decent, Tennessee

They wait, white-haired, chins wagging
both of 'em nagging at ninety.
The home reeks of moth balls and
didn't-*quite*-make-it-to-the-bathroom.
Married sixty years, recliners divided
by one police-band radio
spewing dark chitlins on the rug.
They lap it up like Karo pecan pie.
The dispatcher's nasal crackle
breaks in, enters the room
an invited vandal:
Ten-foot-tall, black male,
breaking and entering . . .
Germantown.

The white woman clutches her gown
around her, imagining
Lord-knows-what-all.
A familiar fear fouls the room,
the vile word *Nigger* darkens
their dentures.

Knock-knock at the back door.
Pop-Paw angles his walker across the floor
to greet the black preacher's wife
from the church across the street
with a holy kiss.
Preacher's wife, Gloria,
brings 'em supper
third night this week,
and homemade meringue-covered
chocolate pie.

They circle the kitchen table
to sup on the sustenance
made by their savior's black body.
They offer a prayer over the blare
of the police-band radio, warn
the preacher's wife
as Pop-Paw cuts the chicken neck
with a razor-sharp knife:
"It's dangerous out there."

Gloria mouths:
"Don't I know it, Lord, don't I know…"

JESUS in Kitties and Flowers

I spy her Watusi-ing
with a weed-whacker,
wielding it like a weapon
on the side of the road
in waist-high grass.
I'm lanced
by her sharp glance —

a safe *seeming* woman
wearing "JESUS"
spelled out in flowers and kitties
across the front of her shirt.

I push-crank my car window
down, cast a simple question
onto her common ground:
"Can you tell me where the
Nazareth, Kentucky
Retreat Center is?"

She cocks her head off to one side,
old eyes, distant, angry and wide.
"Why are you way out *here*
in such a high-class automobile?"

She's suspect of my destination,
voices every single reservation
about the people and the place
where I'm a trying to go.

"There's devil worship
going on up there,
child molestation . . ."
(this woman's got cyclone hair)
". . . sacrifices and other
unspeakable acts."

My car idles on the hairpin turn
while her talk turns to war
and how all we protesters
will burn, burn in hell
at the Nazareth, Kentucky
Retreat Center
up the road.

(Remember now, she's got "JESUS"
spelled in flowers and kitties
across the front of her shirt.)

Before she'll reveal
what I need to know

she wants to make sure
I'm not some homo-
sexual perusing *her* neck
of the woods.

What dawns on me
when her rant is through
is that this poor woman's afraid
of life (and maybe now I am too),
a heart of darkness covered over
by the powerful Prince of Peace.

I'd a left right then,
circling my ear with my finger,
but something about her
caused me to linger:
tarnished dog tags
noosed her neck
like a chain-link fence.

For some odd reason
(I still can't explain it)
I ask her, *Whose tags*?
and then here come her pain:
bloody buckets of soldiers
mowed down
on the side of some road,
her baby boy shipped home
in a pinewood box.

Wind picks up,
our conversation dies down
and it dawns on me
we're on *her* holy ground
and I better back up
and pack up
every judgment
I'm a-hoarding about her.

In this woman's eyes,
wild now, angry and wide,
she's facing the enemy —
ain't nobody on her side
in this gas-guzzling
high-class automobile.

I'm still lanced by her glance
up off the roadside
where she weed-whacked
the waist-high grass.

Aw, Jesus,
kitties and flowers
clinging
for dear life
to the front of her shirt.

*E*verybody I knew called her Aunt Thelma, even her own grown children, like they'd somehow forgotten that she'd been the one to feed, clothe, and shelter 'em. Aside from that, the most memorable thing about her was her dress, drab-gray with a droopy hem. I'm pretty sure Aunt Thelma owned another outfit, though I never saw her wear it. The dress was boxy and loose-fitting on her big body, so much so that my sister and I could have camped under it; that is, if we could have summoned the stamina to withstand the stench. I know it's mean to say, but I always imagined thick slices of rancid rump roast plastered up under each arm of that dark dress—a smell so real you could almost see a colored funk rolling out from the underarm area.

We called my daddy's momma Jebo. Aunt Thelma, Jebo, and I spent many a hot and clammy Saturday morning together crisscrossing Shelby County to visit shut-ins from up at church, delivering green-bean casseroles to people whose family members had passed, and sometimes going up to the funeral home to hug the lost-looking mourners. For such a small community it seemed like a lot of people died pretty regular. Some Saturdays we'd swing by and pick up Jebo's friend, GroverNell, who was not really blood kin to us at all, though we had to call her "Aunt." It would have made more sense to me to call her Uncle GroverNell because of her extremely hairy face.

But let me get back to Aunt Thelma and her B.O. dress. It saturated the air in the rear seat while Jebo's cigarette smoke and White Shoulders perfume fogged up the front. You know how you can walk into somebody's house and it stinks so bad you gag 'cause of their dogs, but the people who live there don't seem to notice the odor? Well, that's how it was with Aunt Thelma in the car beside me in the back. For the first twenty minutes or so I'd have to crane my head down into the neck-hole of my T-shirt to try to filter the stink through the cotton. I will admit that, after driving awhile, I'd finally get used to the smell. I guess it's the same thing as those ladies who work in the beauty shops where hairspray and permanent chemicals hang so thick you can't see; I've watched them talk, laugh, and smoke like "What's the big deal?" Plus, Jebo would instruct me to "Offer it up to the Lord," adding that if my Uncle John could work at the dead fish factory, I could ride in the same car with Aunt Thelma.

After our errands were done, and we'd had a nice sack lunch of bologna sandwiches and Charles Chips on the side of the road, Jebo would drive everyone back home. GroverNell liked to be dropped off first so she could watch her favorite television programs, then finally we'd take Aunt Thelma home, way out on Deadfall Road.

Watching her hoist herself from the car and walk up the long gravel driveway back to the house, I couldn't quit thinking about her dress. There was a certain sorrow to it. I'd never asked her much about herself, but the older I get the more interested in her I become. One day, I might just sneak into that tiny back bedroom and find the chair she put it on to air it out at night. If the blinds are drawn, the open neck of that drab-gray dress might look like a gaping mouth. Maybe I could sit down and talk to that dress, and maybe the dress would talk back. I might even hold it in my arms and rock it with a love right out of Matthew Mark Luke and John. Over time that dress would wear out completely, just like her old earthly body. I'm drawn to the sorrow it's seen. I can only imagine the stories it would tell.

Mourning the Missionaries

Fay's shingles flare
every time she imagines Janith Gay
over there in Ro-mania.
Crimson whelps itch; she scratches.
Misery mounts as she mourns
the tender times between them.

They bound Bibles in boxes
to send ahead to the new church.
No hot water; grandbaby bottoms
raw against Sears paper —
Fay conjures despair,
flicks ashes off her Winston
onto the desert floor of her empty house.

Gonna be a missionary.
Yeah I hear you.
Called to do the Lord's work . . . sshhhtt.
Taking my daughter off to God knows where
two weeks after the wedding.
Fay flies into another itching fit.
Digs for a lighter and Calamine lotion,
applies both.

What'd I do wrong? cries Fay.
Janith Gay—a saint now
going over that-a-way,
carrying all out Baptist hopes,
missionary-style, overseas.

More than any of the rest of us
ever done.

If Only, Aunt Sye

You walk year-miles behind a gray mule
staring deep into a black hole.
Men all off at war, or stinking drunk, one.
You plow damp earth over and under,
over and under. Hands weep
openly at night by the small fire,
knitting covers for the beds.
Hopes of children wash out
with the next moon, soiled sheets.

Wayne swears he won't wait any longer.
Begs, "Come with me, Sye." You shrug,
toss the graying braid across your shoulder.
"Got to store plow-mules before barn-dark."

"There's time to bathe," he pleads.
"Comb your hair; wear that cotton dress—
makes your green eyes shine."
If only.
If only we'd canned on time.
Would you have taken his hand,
river-walked that night?

Oh, but the hoot owls taunted:
Who, who will feed your family?
Sister's down, always down with the blues.
They'll starve, starve, every one of them, starve.

That garden fed us.
The young'uns thrived.
One of them bore a daughter: me.
Every Sunday we eat fried okra,
fresh field peas, sliced tomatoes.
We all clasp hands and bless this family
your food sustained.

Grace on the Fourth of July

Firecrackers split hot air
above the yard on Frayser Boulevard.
A pack of wild relatives in from Little Rock
spell their names with sparklers
in the afternoon sky.
Whooping and hollering,
devouring barbecue, vultures
circle to see who's divorced whom.
Lady, a two-tone shepherd tied at the stake,
strains against her chain.
Cussing second cousins slurp
cold watermelon, spit seeds.
Two, dressed in police uniforms,
pepper-spray the driveway.
The rest ride barrels in Memphis rodeos.
Aunts, great and caretaker weary,
make iced tea toasts to cooler days.

Stories, snippets in collage, pile
one on top of the other:
"How's the store, Noble?"
        "You should've sued."
"Tomatoes look good."
        "We've been meaning to
                ever since her birthday."

The woman
in a soft white-haired bun,
twisted carefully and pinned
to the private part of her neck,
stands out a mile in this crowd.
I know she raised my grandmother
when her own family'd given her away.
Graceful across the grass,
replenishing the table—

God's own wedding china
in a sea of paper plates.

I want one word: Welcome. I want her waiting outside in the yard for us wearing, of all things, a freshly washed rubber-waisted pantsuit, maybe lemon yellow with white rickrack around the squareish neck, when we all pull up into the drive to her small brick house off Highway 50. I make her, in my mind, somehow smother all six of us in her lard-laden arms, happy as a lark, maybe hiding a gift from her volunteer job at Clothes Closet behind her back for only me. My imagination can cook up quite a greeting if I let it. But the pictures in my head give way to real life; I wrestle the memories.

First off, it's hot and near dark. The long, hot, no-air-conditioning ride across the flat scrub land of West Tennessee wilts us. In the backseat my sister and I ball up fists and beat each other pretty much the whole way. Daddy always takes the Jackson Bypass to visit his momma on the way home from Memphis. When we get there, there's a slight peel-off sound as my stuck legs release the plastic seat and struggle to get a walk in motion. I am forever struck by the way my shadow of a grandmother always answers the porch screen door. Jebo, a tiny crunked-over woman, answers as though our intrusive headlights turning in after dusk are the bright blades of burglars' flashlights. Armored head to toe in a grease-splattered flower-print apron and serving spoon, she cracks open the door hissing: "Who are you and what do you want?" Thunderstruck from the storm sound of her words, I latch onto the street side of my sister, struggling to come up with an answer.

"Uh, it's your grandchildren, Jebo, and we sure could use a drink of water."

But her question, slipped through the open crack of a country shack, somehow doesn't seem fully answered.

Who are we and what do we want?

I catch the familiar smell of over-cooked turnip greens wafting through the screen. She wears her pot likker like fufu water.

Our funny child faces soften her and our names work as password. Next thing I know the door is wide open. Once inside, the scent of freezer corn and sweet potatoes soak the air. I know her question, slow to evaporate, still hangs in the humidity where night meets porch-light at the threshold.

"Who are you and what do you want?"

Suddenly I'm certain who I am and what I want are two very different things.

What I want is her waiting in the kitchen wearing, of all things, a freshly pinned Easter orchid corsage with baby's-breath garnish and a feathered fern backing at her breast, when we all barge in bearing pink ribboned baskets and still-hot weave-top peach pies.

Put Her to Rest

Three days after the fried pie funeral
he calls me to come clean
out her closet, a cedar-lined mausoleum.
Crammed in the corner: the long-sleeved
duster she wore all winter —
mopping floors, washing dishes, rolling hair.

I stuff my too-green memories
like straw down the sleeves
of the scarecrow dress
until my savior's coat hanger
becomes a cross I'll hang
in the corner of my fields
to scare the caw off crows

that threaten my sleep.

Speak to Me, Tennessee

Eighty-seven years old, tall as a tree.
Eye to eye we stare silently
squatting by the wall heater.
Oh speak to me,
Speak
Tennessee.

Her pale, dusty scalp shines;
no, it mumbles through old hair.
I want to rub my hand there
and against the wiry fuzz
beneath her heavy stockings
to make her real again.

Her mouth widens out
to mostly anchored teeth
when the grandkids show up.
Pink powder keeps house
in her crevassed face.
Triceps, a memory,
the skin puckered,
lotioned, and droopy.

Tennessee's a teetotaler
when it comes to liquor,
unlike her living sister, Thelma
with stories of housing-project
whiskey parties
and falling flat on the floor
that night she survived the fire.

Tennessee applies blue rinse
on Saturday night
before Sunday church.
Tennessee drives her own
Chevrolet, a straw hat on display
through the back window.

I taste her dust as they drive her away.

Speak to me,
Speak
Tennessee.

Desperate Ransom

At five, my magical mind
borrowed a single thread from Time
to try and mend a rent sky, the big blue hole
Mee Maw tore through in order to
Sitteth at the right hand of the Father.
My ransom was handfuls
of sock-saved birthday money
offered up from pink palms to a silent God.
I begged, "Give her back, please give her back,"
an empty echo sound rattling in my piggy bank.

Today the payment is my own name
ricocheting off the walls of this vein-blue room
as I sort through the scattered snippets
of old stories and poems.
I'm finally willing to set them free,
an overnight jar of lightning bugs
thrown into the bright light of day,
the toll for taking the hard way
across a rusty bed of nails.

There's a frightened willingness
to kick over the brash boulder
hunkered down in the middle of this
dung-brindle shag-carpet living room.
The rock will cry out, braying like a mule
'til you give it room to bear witness to what it's seen.
It demands a desperate ransom:
the weight of all that rubble, the big story,
all the trouble you hold onto
until finally, leg-weary and wavering,
you fork it over and stride on, spine-straight,
into the business of living your one true life.

$\mathcal{T}$here you have it. The truth of who we are, of who I am, hung out to dry on the line of the evening's heat. If it weren't for that floor fan blowing, we'd have burned up in here. Looks like everybody's getting ready to push away from the table. I want to sit a second and bask in the loud silence surrounding us.

In just a little bit, my people will scrape the food from their plates and pile up dishes in the stainless steel sink for somebody else to wash, rinse, and towel dry. What's left of the fried corn, field peas, sliced tomatoes, pork chops, and corn bread will be scooped out of pots and pans, sealed away in plastic containers for another time.

Some of us may wander around looking lost, hovering like hungry ghosts; others will wear a satisfied smile, having briefly known the deep satisfaction reserved for those who've been carefully listened to. Though I try, I can't keep Aunt Fay from snuffing out her cigarette in a half-eaten pile of mashed potatoes.

Thank you for coming to the table. There's much more to tell—more rooms to explore in the house of Who I Am. And maybe you'll come again, tell your stories. The simple fact of the matter is that we might all tell our stories if someone would just hear us out, hear us with a kind ear until we feel safe enough to speak.

Don't run off, now; y'all might want to stay for dessert. I hear Momma hollering for me to help her with the coffee.

Acknowledgments

I would like to thank my family members, every one of them, especially John, Jonas, and Liza, as well as Mom, Dad, Greg, Ginger, and Kristi. My deepest gratitude to Nikki, George, Molly, and Eve for all of their guidance in this process, and a huge thank-you to my editor, friend, and partner in this grace-filled crime of poetry, Kelly Falzone. Many thanks as well to Ami McConnell and the folks at WestBow Press for coming out to the shows and making this book a possibility.

A big round of applause and admiration goes out to the brilliant musicians I've had the joy of collaborating with over the years. Inspired by them, I've traveled more deeply into the musicality of these words. Although the poems show up here without a soundtrack, the music and inspiration of each still shows up on the page. Thanks to Rob Jackson, John Jackson, Steve Conn, Chris Thile, Keb' Mo', Darrell Scott, Marcus Hummon, Maura O'Connell, and Pat Flynn. Thanks to the Davis family for inspiring Tornado Drawers.

Special thanks, also, to everyone who's come out to my live shows and asked for a written account of my performances—this is for you. And finally, thanks to theologian Dr. Peggy Way for framing for me the questions undergirding this beautiful, perilous journey called life: Who can we trust? Who we are supposed to be? How do we make meaning of it all? and How can we live together peacefully on this planet?

For more on Minton Sparks,
visit her website at www.mintonsparks.com